I AM READING

HOCUS-POCUS Hound

SAMANTHA HAY

ILLUSTRATED BY

NATHAN REED

KINGFISHER

BOSTON

For Alice

KINGFISHER
a Houghton Mifflin Company imprint
222 Berkeley Street
Boston, Massachusetts 02116
www.houghtonmifflinbooks.com

First published in 2006
2 4 6 8 10 9 7 5 3 1

LIBRARY OF CONGRESS CATALOGING-IN-PUBLICATION DATA
has been applied for.

ISBN-13: 978-0-7534-5957-7
ISBN-10: 0-7534-5957-4

Printed in China
1TR/0506/WKT/SCHOY/115MA/C

Contents

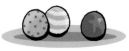
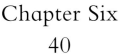

Chapter One

Marvo the magician was in a bad mood.

He was trying out his latest trick.

But it wasn't working very well.

"Stop fidgeting!" he shouted at his assistant, Doris.

She was sitting inside a big box with just her head popping out from the top, while Marvo tried to stick swords through the side.

"Sit still!" he thundered.

But Doris couldn't sit still. She'd gulped down three extra-large milk shakes at lunchtime.

"Um . . . Marvo," she said, "I think
I need to use the bathroom!"
Marvo threw down the swords.
"Nincompoop! You're the worst
assistant in the whole world!"

Poor Doris.
She wasn't a very
good magician's
assistant.
She mixed up
the magic cards . . .

. . . and
misplaced the
magic wand.

And whenever she was sawed in half, she'd fidget and squirm. (Secretly, she was a little bit worried that Marvo might decide not to put her back together again!)

Marvo had had enough.

He yanked open the stage door.

"Follow me!" he shouted.

"The first person I see when I leave this theater will be my new assistant!"

But, luckily for Doris, the street was empty . . . except for a shaggy old dog eating scraps from a trash can.

"He'll do!" bellowed Marvo.

Doris was astonished.

"You can't have an old dog as your
assistant," she said with a gasp.

But Marvo had decided.

The old dog was his new assistant.

Chapter Two

The dog was ugly.

He was big and shaggy with gray whiskers. And his coat was the color of mud.

Actually, it wasn't just the color of mud. It WAS mud! But Doris did her best with a large sponge and some of Marvo's shampoo.

The dog also had very bad breath,
long toenails, and a gas problem.
But Marvo didn't care—because the old
dog was surprisingly smart!

So, while Doris sat and scrubbed rabbit
droppings out of Marvo's top hat, the
dog learned some tricks.

He learned card
tricks, hard tricks,
and stand-on-a-
box-and-fly tricks.

He learned to
juggle with rings
and do tricks
with string.

He learned to pull flowers out of his ears and balance hard-boiled eggs on his tail.
He never mixed up the magic cards or misplaced the magic wand.
And he certainly never squirmed when he was being sawed in half.

Marvo was delighted. "Who says you can't teach an old dog new tricks?" he boomed.

"I will call him my Hocus-Pocus Hound!" The dog wagged his tail excitedly. Then his bottom made a noise.

"People will come from near and far to see him!" said Marvo, holding his nose. And they did.

"Marvo the Magician and his Hocus-Pocus Hound" was a sellout!

"He's a million times better than you were!" bragged Marvo to Doris. "And I don't even have to pay him!"

Doris didn't mind. She'd never liked being Marvo's assistant anyway. And she'd always wanted a dog. Whenever Marvo wasn't looking, she'd switch the cheap cans of dog food that Marvo bought for extra-expensive, supersize sausages.

Hocus-Pocus Hound
was delighted.

Doris had a pet.

And Marvo had
lots of money.
And that's where
the tale might have
ended . . . mostly
happily ever after.
But then . . .
Marvo got greedy.

Chapter Three

One night, just before he and
Hocus-Pocus Hound went onstage,
Marvo went to find Doris.

She was in the dressing room, shining
Marvo's shoes.

"I've decided that I don't need you
anymore!" he told her. "You're fired!"

Doris was stunned. "But who'll iron your cape and polish the wands?"

"Hocus-Pocus Hound, of course!" said Marvo. "I can teach him how to do anything."

But Hocus-Pocus Hound, who was listening at the door, didn't like the sound of that!

He narrowed his eyes and growled.

But Marvo wasn't finished.

"And I know all about the sausages!" snapped Marvo. "I'll be taking the cost of them out of your last paycheck!" And, with that, he swept out of the dressing room.

Doris was miserable.

With a heavy heart, she started to pack.

Meanwhile, Marvo and Hocus-Pocus
Hound went onstage.

It was their best show ever.

Hocus-Pocus Hound was on top form.

He balanced on a ball while pulling

a cat out of a top hat.

Most daring of all, Hocus-Pocus
Hound allowed himself to be
successfully sawed, not in half—but
in eighths.

The audience was delighted.

Oooh!

But Marvo wasn't finished yet.

Chapter Four

"Tonight," boomed Marvo to the
audience, "my Hocus-Pocus Hound
will attempt a new trick—he will
make ME disappear!"
The lights were dimmed.

The audience was silent.

Marvo stepped inside a big green box.
He waved to the audience and then
pulled the door shut behind him.
Hocus-Pocus Hound—beautifully
turned out in a top hat and his tail—
picked up Marvo's magic wand in his
mouth and trotted over to the box.
He bowed to the audience and then
waved the wand three times in front of
the box.

There was a puff of pink smoke, a
crash of thunder, and a faint smell of
rotten eggs.

And, suddenly, the door of the box
creaked open. It was empty.

Marvo wasn't there. He'd completely disappeared!
The audience was impressed.
There was thunderous applause.
People were on their feet.

Oooooh!

Hocus-Pocus Hound wagged his tail.

The audience cheered.

Hocus-Pocus Hound wagged his

tail again.

The audience cheered some more.

But then, slowly, the cheering and the clapping stopped as the audience waited for Hocus-Pocus Hound to bring back Marvo.

But he didn't.

Instead, he laid down on the stage and went to sleep.

Chapter Five

The audience pointed and whispered
and shuffled in their seats.

The theater manager bit his nails and
scratched his head.

But Marvo still didn't reappear.

Hocus-Pocus Hound was now snoring.

There was only one person who could
help. Doris!

The theater manager rushed off to
find her.

"Quick, Doris! You've got to come!"
he said, bursting into the dressing room.

But Doris had her coat on.

She'd packed her suitcase and was
ready to leave.

"You can't go!" begged the theater
manager. "Hocus-Pocus Hound has
made Marvo disappear, and I don't
think he wants to bring him back!"
Doris tried not to laugh.

She liked the idea of a world without
Marvo, but however much she disliked
him, she didn't want the audience to
go home disappointed.

Doris followed the manager back to
the stage. They found Hocus-Pocus
Hound still fast asleep.
The audience was shuffling, and some
people were starting to leave.
"Wake up,
Hocus-Pocus
Hound!" said
Doris, tickling
his ears.
Nothing
happened.

"Sausages!" whispered Doris.

But still Hocus-Pocus Hound slept on.

The theater manager was wringing his

hands with worry.

Doris suddenly had an idea.

She took off Hocus-Pocus Hound's top

hat and slipped it on her own head.

Then she whisked off her coat and

turned to the audience.

"Ladies and gentleman!" she shouted.
"Please take your seats for the return
of the great Marvo the magician!"
Then she picked up Marvo's magic
wand.

She knew all of Marvo's magic words!
She just hoped that she'd remember
them in the right order.

After all, she didn't want to turn

Marvo into a mouse or a frog . . .

(well, not really!)

She took a deep breath.

Then she waved the magic wand three

times in front of the empty green box.

Chapter Six

PHWOOOPH!

There was a puff of pink smoke, a
crash of thunder, and a faint smell
of cheese.

Then, suddenly, the door of the box
swung open . . .

. . . and there was Marvo—

a very angry-looking Marvo!

"Wow!" said Doris. "I've done it!"

"Hooray!" shouted the audience.

They cheered and clapped so loudly

that they woke up Hocus-Pocus Hound.

The audience was delighted.

People cheered and clapped and
clapped and cheered, until finally the
curtain came down and everything
was quiet.

Marvo turned to Doris and Hocus-Pocus
Hound with a face like thunder.

He opened his mouth to yell at them . . .

. . . when he noticed that Hocus-Pocus Hound had picked up his magic wand and was waving it angrily.

Doris had the same tough look on her face as Hocus-Pocus Hound.

Marvo suddenly felt a little bit shaky.

His knees began to knock.

His throat felt dry.

He'd been lost in the green box for a long time, and he didn't like the idea of a repeat performance!

"Um . . . Doris," he said, "how would you like to be my assistant again?"

Doris blushed. "I'd love to!" she said.

"But what about Hocus-Pocus Hound?"

"You can both be my assistants!" said Marvo, looking nervously at Hocus-Pocus Hound. "I think maybe two heads might be better than one!"

Everyone was happy.

Even with Hocus-Pocus Hound's help,
Doris sometimes still mixed up the
magic cards and misplaced the magic
wand. But Marvo didn't shout at her
when she did.

Because Marvo knew that, if he got even
the slightest bit angry, Hocus–Pocus
Hound would give him a stern stare
and a wave of the wand.

And Marvo knew what that meant . . .

About the author and illustrator

Samantha Hay trained as a journalist and spent ten years working in television. She now looks after her little girl and writes children's stories. She lives in Wales. *Hocus-Pocus Hound* is her second book for Kingfisher.

"I'd love to be a magician," says Sam. "But unfortunately the only trick I know is how to make chocolate disappear!"

Nathan Reed has had a love for creating characters ever since drawing in the sand with his dad on vacation. He has been illustrating children's books since graduating from Falmouth College of Arts in 2000.

"Although my own dog, Sam, is very clever," says Nathan, "I don't think he could ever perform tricks quite like Hocus-Pocus Hound!"

Strategies for Independent Readers

Predict

Think about the cover, illustrations, and the title of the book. What do you think this book will be about? While you are reading think about what may happen next and why.

Monitor

As you read ask yourself if what you're reading makes sense. If it doesn't, reread, look at the illustrations, or read ahead.

Question

Ask yourself questions about important ideas in the story such as what the characters might do or what you might learn.

Phonics

If there is a word that you do not know, look carefully at the letters, sounds, and word parts that you do know. Blend the sounds to read the word. Ask yourself if this is a word you know. Does it make sense in the sentence?

Summarize

Think about the characters, the setting where the story takes place, and the problem the characters faced in the story. Tell the important ideas in the beginning, middle, and end of the story.

Evaluate

Ask yourself questions like: Did you like the story? Why or why not? How did the author make the story come alive? How did the author make the story fun to read? How well did you understand the story? Maybe you can understand it better if you read it again!